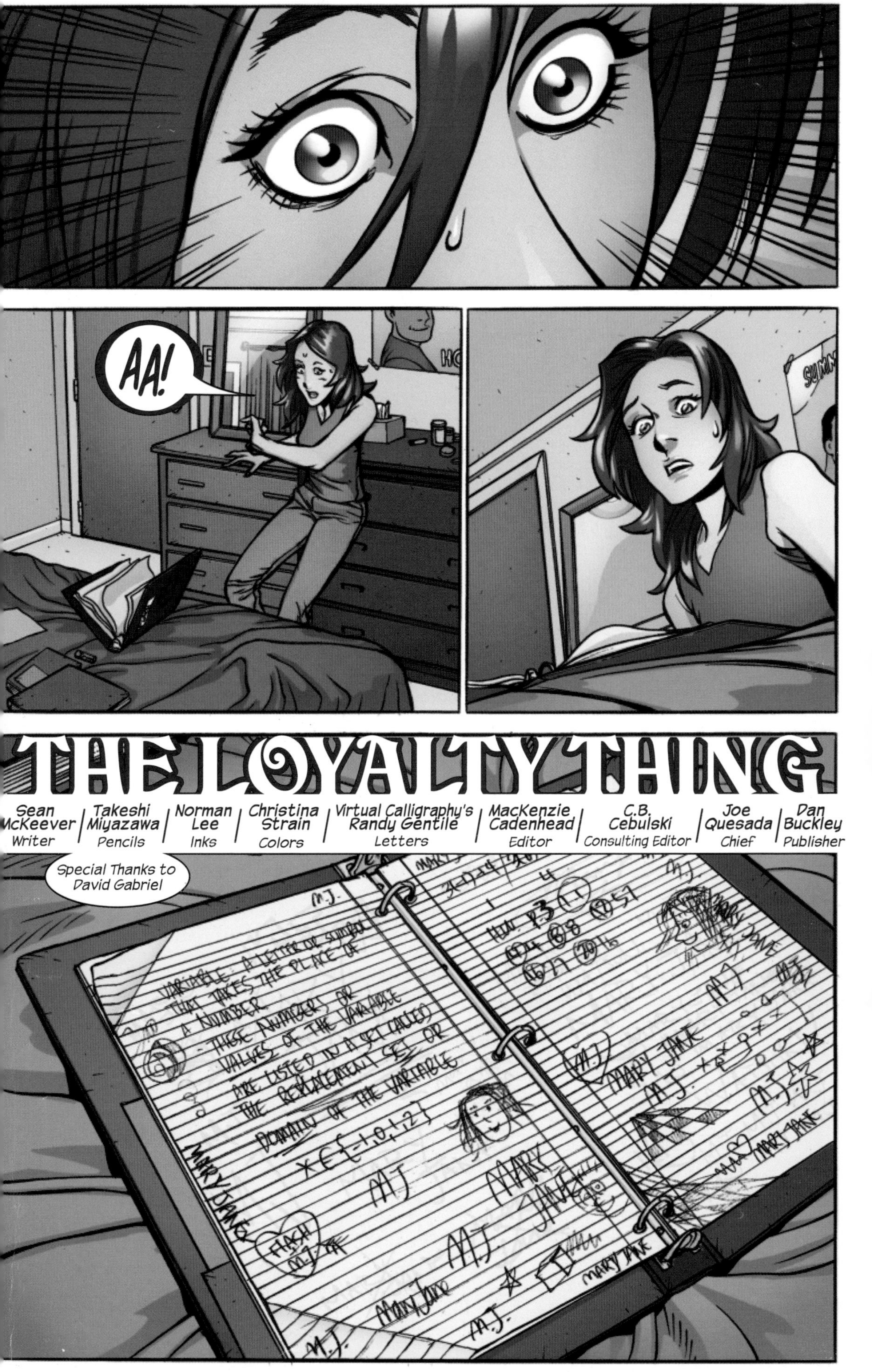

AA!
THE LOYALTY THING
Sean McKeever Writer
Takeshi Miyazawa Pencils
Norman Lee Inks
Christina Strain Colors
Virtual Calligraphy's Randy Gentile Letters
MacKenzie Cadenhead Editor
C.B. Cebulski Consulting Editor
Joe Quesada Chief
Dan Buckley Publisher
Special Thanks to David Gabriel

VISIT US AT

www.abdopub.com

Spotlight, a division of ABDO Publishing Company Inc., is the school and library distributor of the Marvel Entertainment books.

Library bound edition © 2006

Library of Congress Cataloging-in-Publication Data

The Loyalty Thing

ISBN 1-59961-037-X

All Spotlight books are reinforced library binding and manufactured in the United States of America

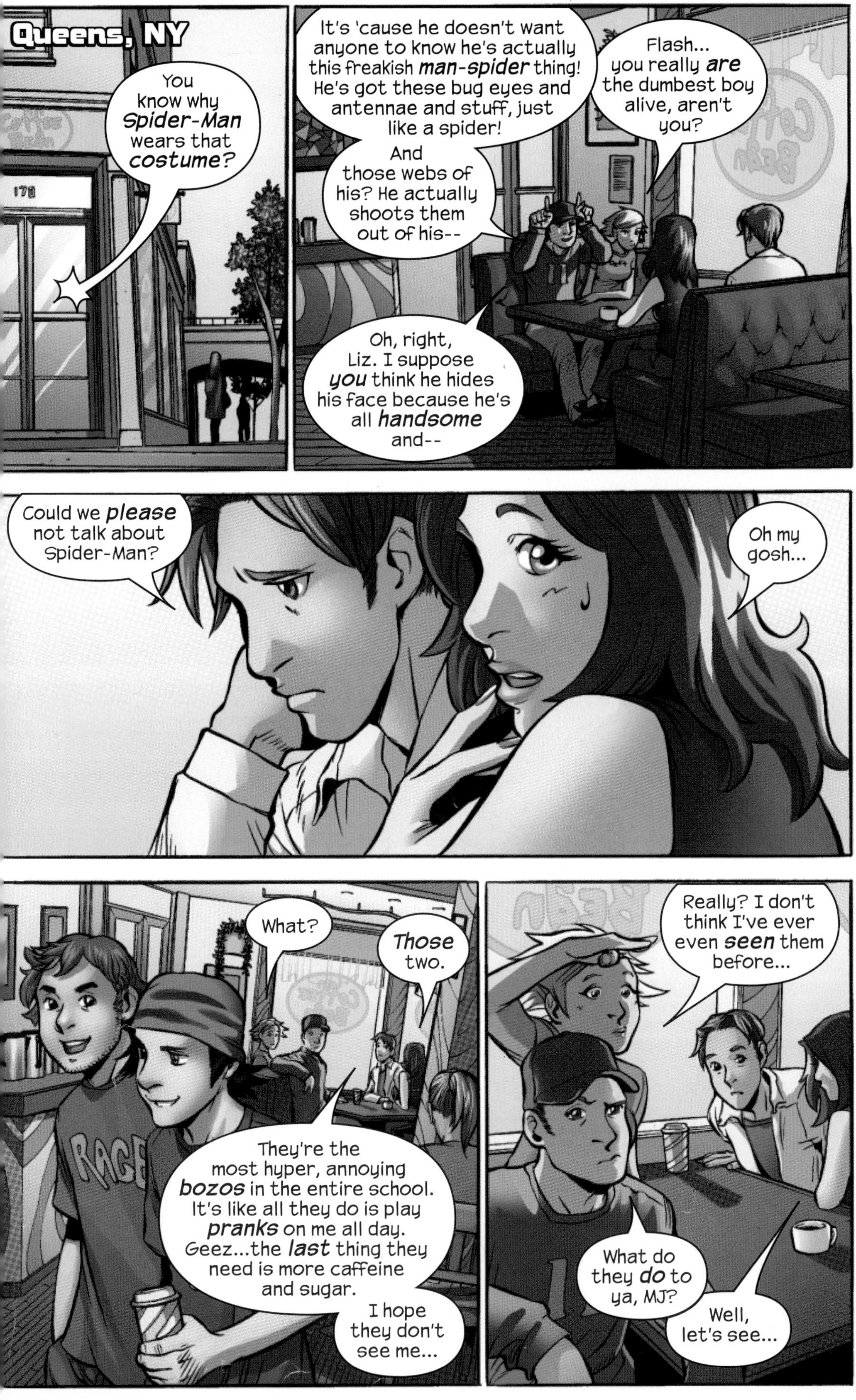
Queens, NY
You know why Spider-Man wears that costume?
It's 'cause he doesn't want anyone to know he's actually this freakish man-spider thing! He's got these bug eyes and antennae and stuff, just like a spider!
And those webs of his? He actually shoots them out of his--
Flash... you really are the dumbest boy alive, aren't you?
Oh, right, Liz. I suppose you think he hides his face because he's all handsome and--
Could we please not talk about Spider-Man?
Oh my gosh...
What?
Those two.
They're the most hyper, annoying bozos in the entire school. It's like all they do is play pranks on me all day. Geez...the last thing they need is more caffeine and sugar.
I hope they don't see me...
Really? I don't think I've ever even seen them before...
What do they do to ya, MJ?
Well, let's see...

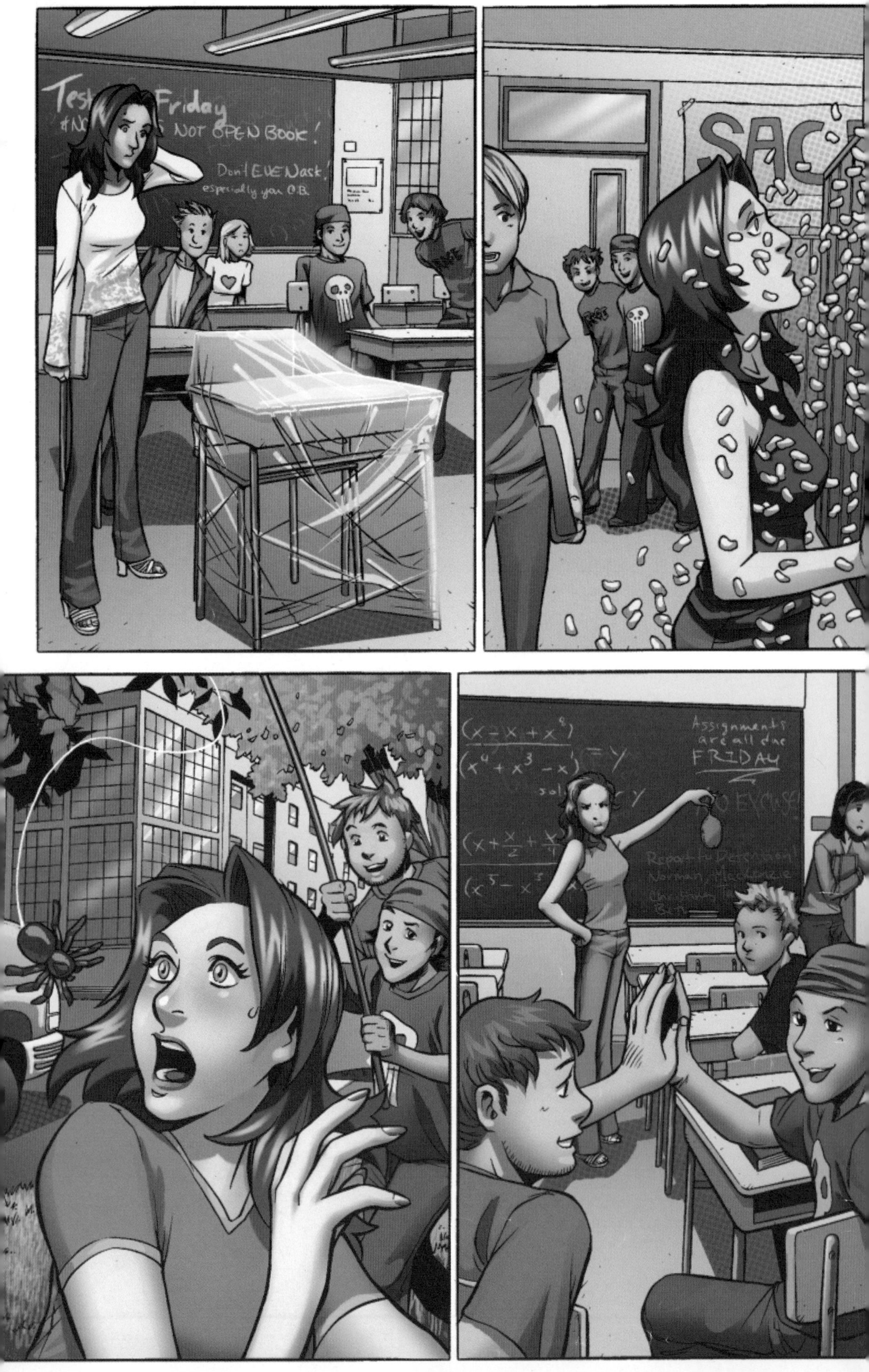
Friday
NOT OPEN Book!
Don't EVEN ask!
especially you C.B.
Assignments are all due FRIDAY

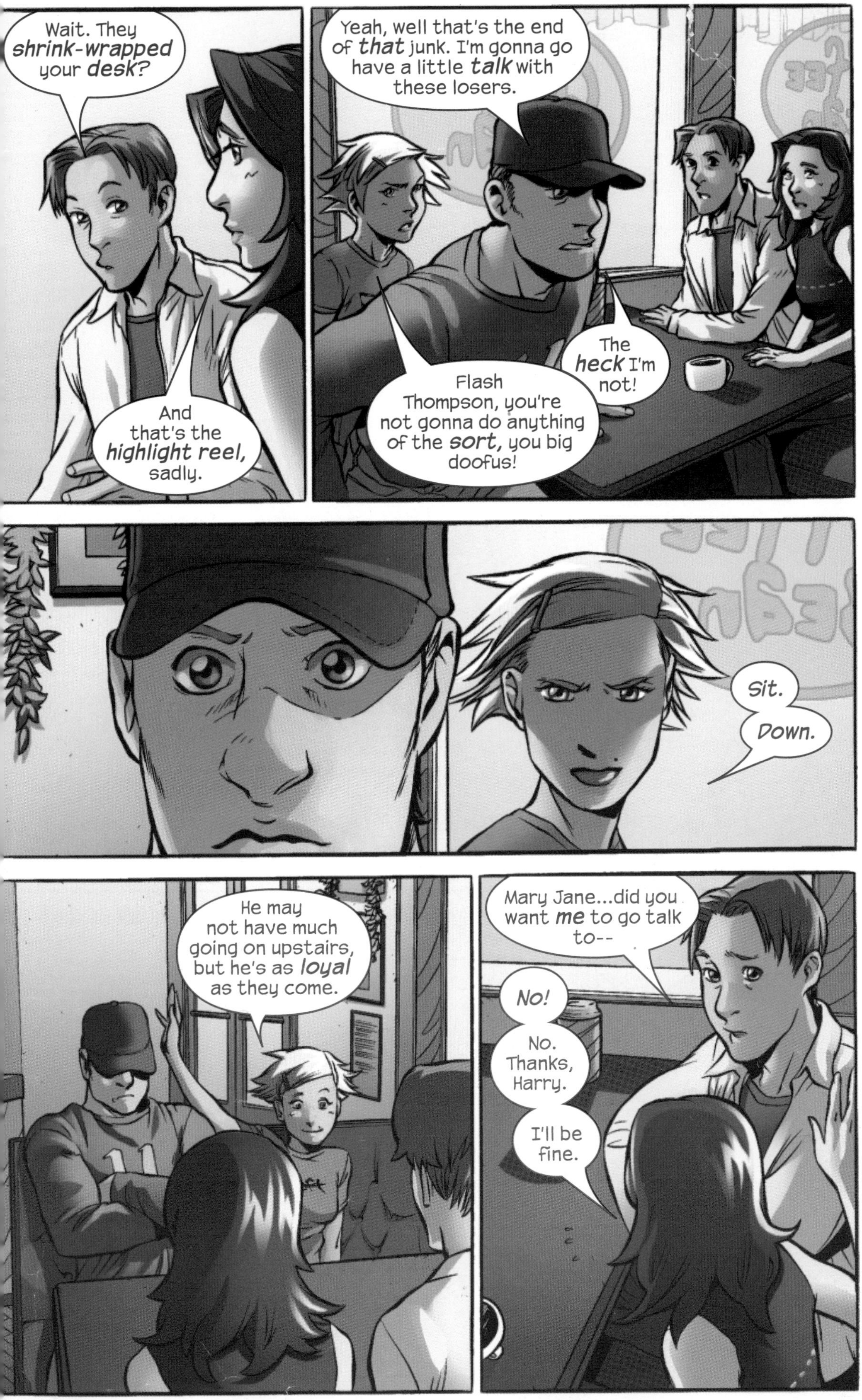
Wait. They shrink-wrapped your desk?
And that's the highlight reel, sadly.
Yeah, well that's the end of that junk. I'm gonna go have a little talk with these losers.
Flash Thompson, you're not gonna do anything of the sort, you big doofus!
The heck I'm not!
Sit.
Down.
He may not have much going on upstairs, but he's as loyal as they come.
Mary Jane...did you want me to go talk to--
No!
No. Thanks, Harry.
I'll be fine.

So, MJ...what's the *story* with those guys?

How should *I* know? It's not like I ever *did* anything to them.

I know! You're an *angel.* You're a sweetheart!

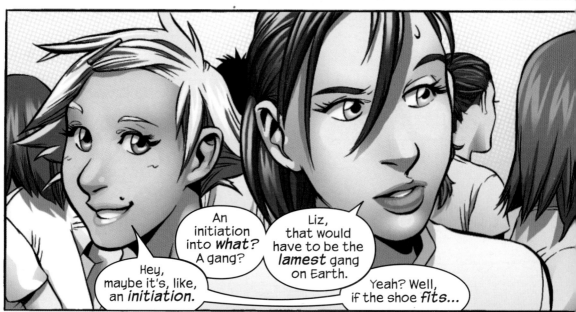

An initiation into *what?* A gang?

Liz, that would have to be the *lamest* gang on Earth.

Hey, maybe it's, like, an *initiation.*

Yeah? Well, if the shoe *fits...*

Har har.

Love ya!

FWEET!

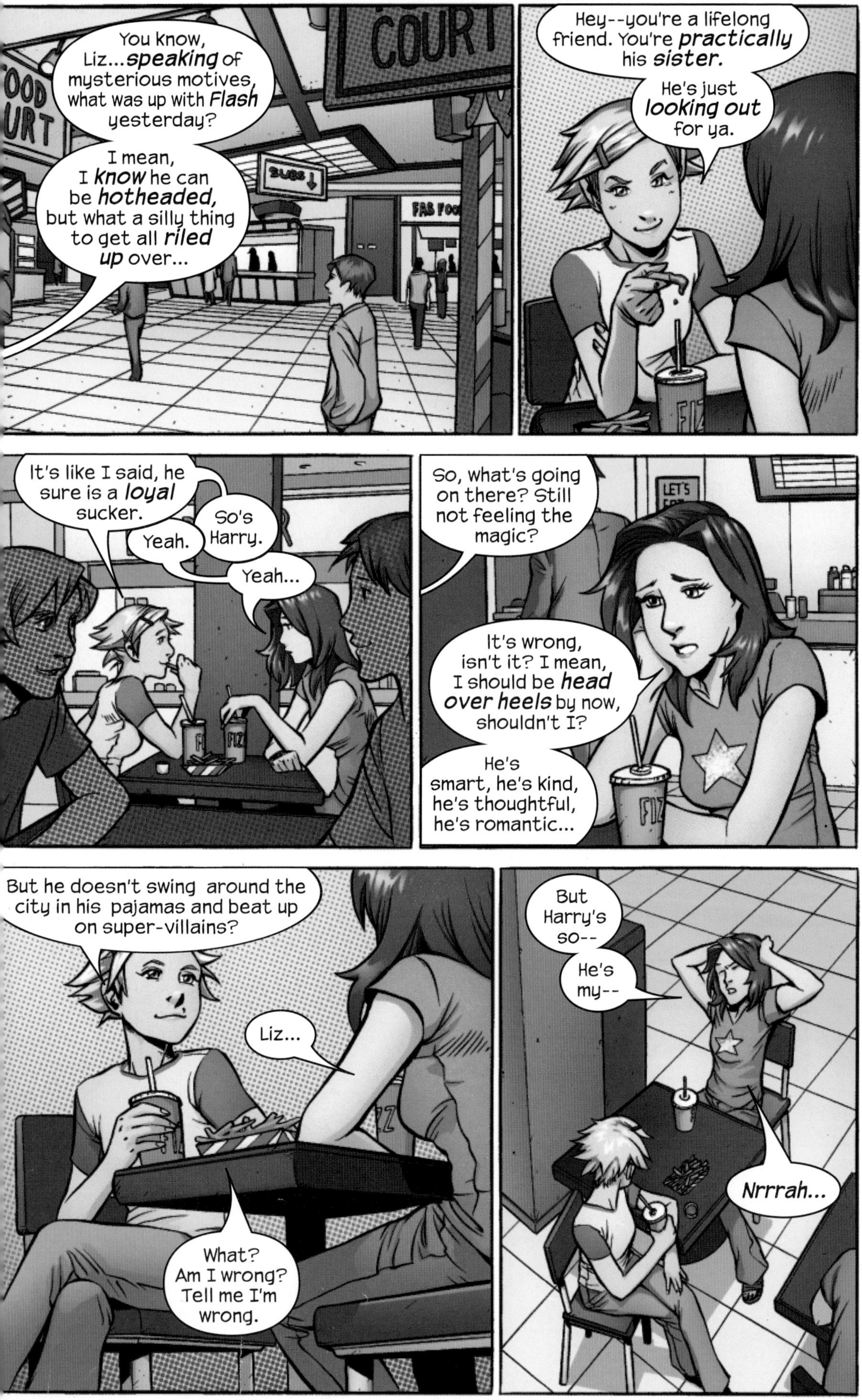

You know, Liz...speaking of mysterious motives, what was up with Flash yesterday?
I mean, I know he can be hotheaded, but what a silly thing to get all riled up over...
Hey--you're a lifelong friend. You're practically his sister.
He's just looking out for ya.
It's like I said, he sure is a loyal sucker.
Yeah.
So's Harry.
Yeah...
So, what's going on there? Still not feeling the magic?
It's wrong, isn't it? I mean, I should be head over heels by now, shouldn't I?
He's smart, he's kind, he's thoughtful, he's romantic...
But he doesn't swing around the city in his pajamas and beat up on super-villains?
Liz...
What? Am I wrong? Tell me I'm wrong.
But Harry's so--
He's my--
Nrrrah...

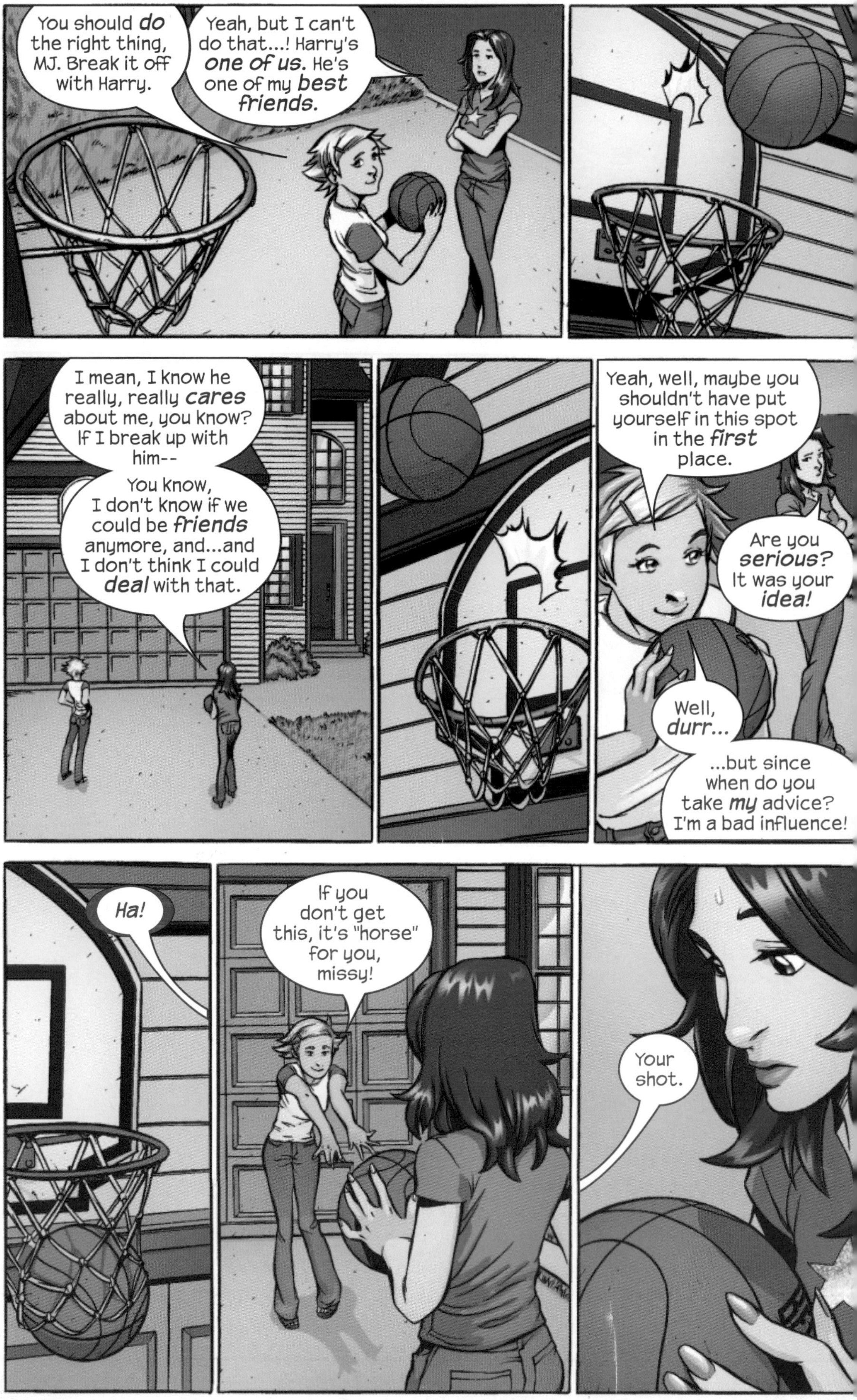
You should do the right thing, MJ. Break it off with Harry.
Yeah, but I can't do that...! Harry's one of us. He's one of my best friends.
I mean, I know he really, really cares about me, you know? If I break up with him--
You know, I don't know if we could be friends anymore, and...and I don't think I could deal with that.
Yeah, well, maybe you shouldn't have put yourself in this spot in the first place.
Are you serious? It was your idea!
Well, durr...
...but since when do you take my advice? I'm a bad influence!
Ha!
If you don't get this, it's "horse" for you, missy!
Your shot.

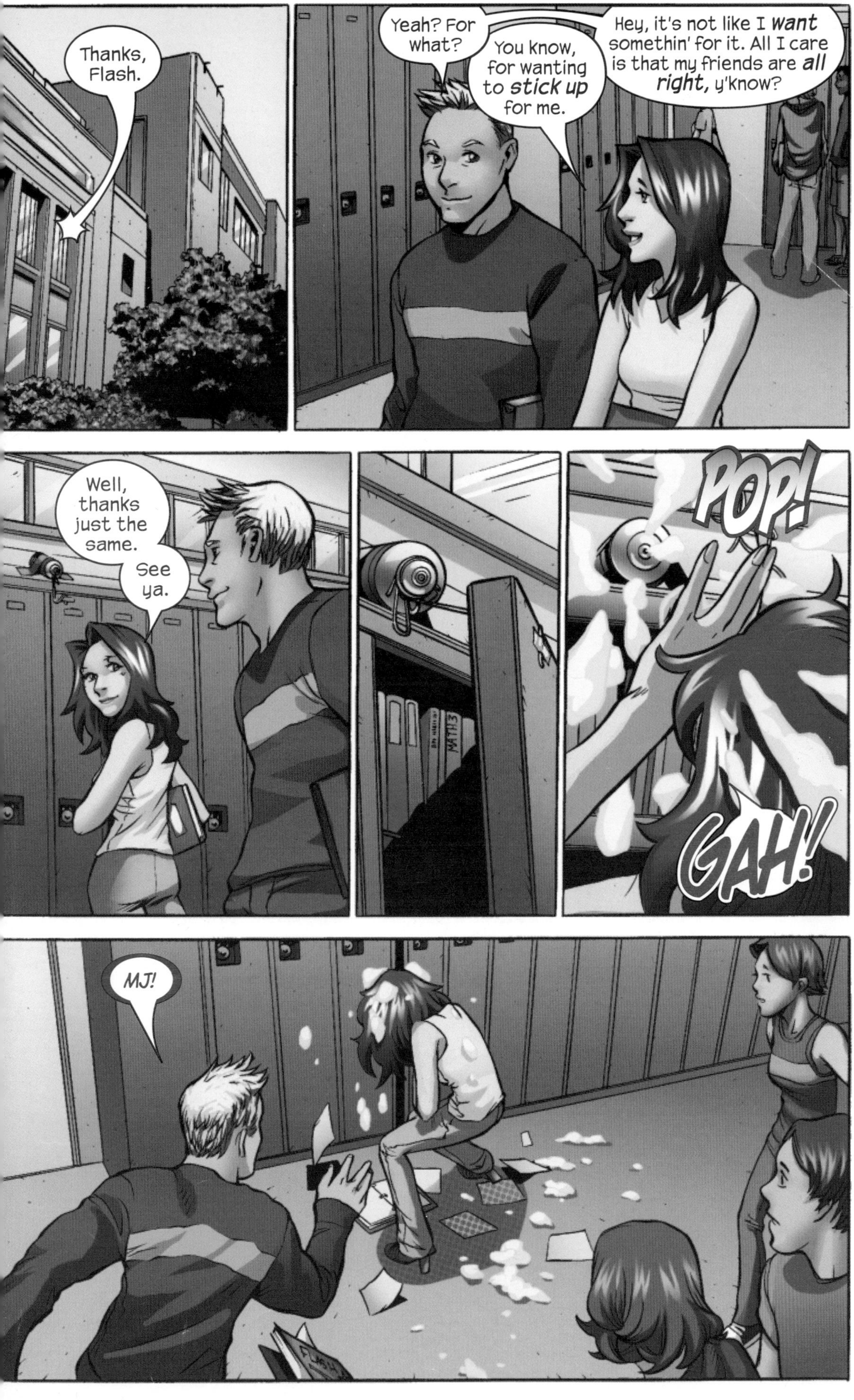

Thanks, Flash.
Yeah? For what?
You know, for wanting to *stick up* for me.
Hey, it's not like I *want* somethin' for it. All I care is that my friends are *all right,* y'know?
Well, thanks just the same.
See ya.
POP!
GAH!
MJ!

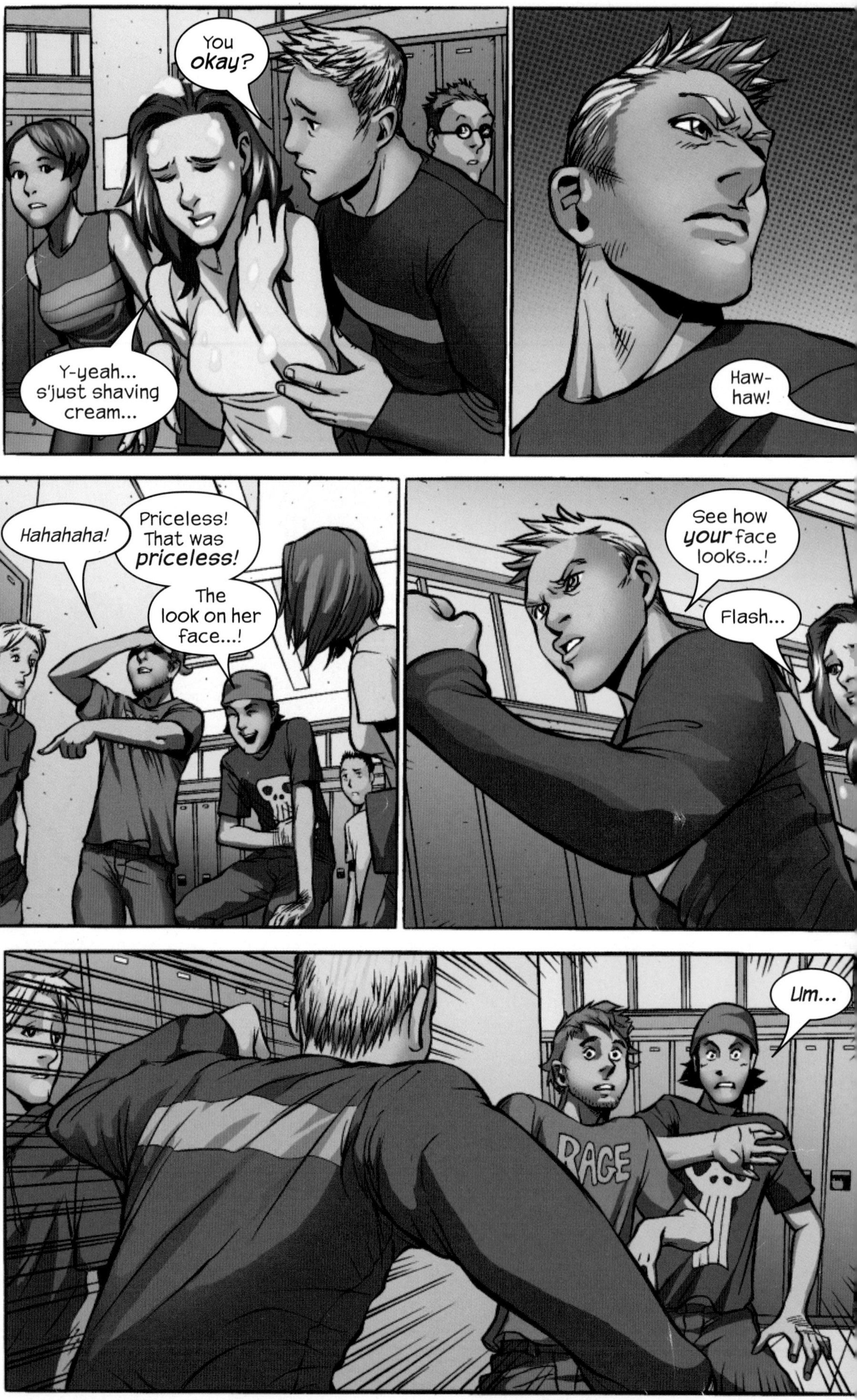
You okay?
Y-yeah... s'just shaving cream...
Haw-haw!
Hahahaha!
Priceless! That was priceless!
The look on her face...!
See how your face looks...!
Flash...
Um...
RACE

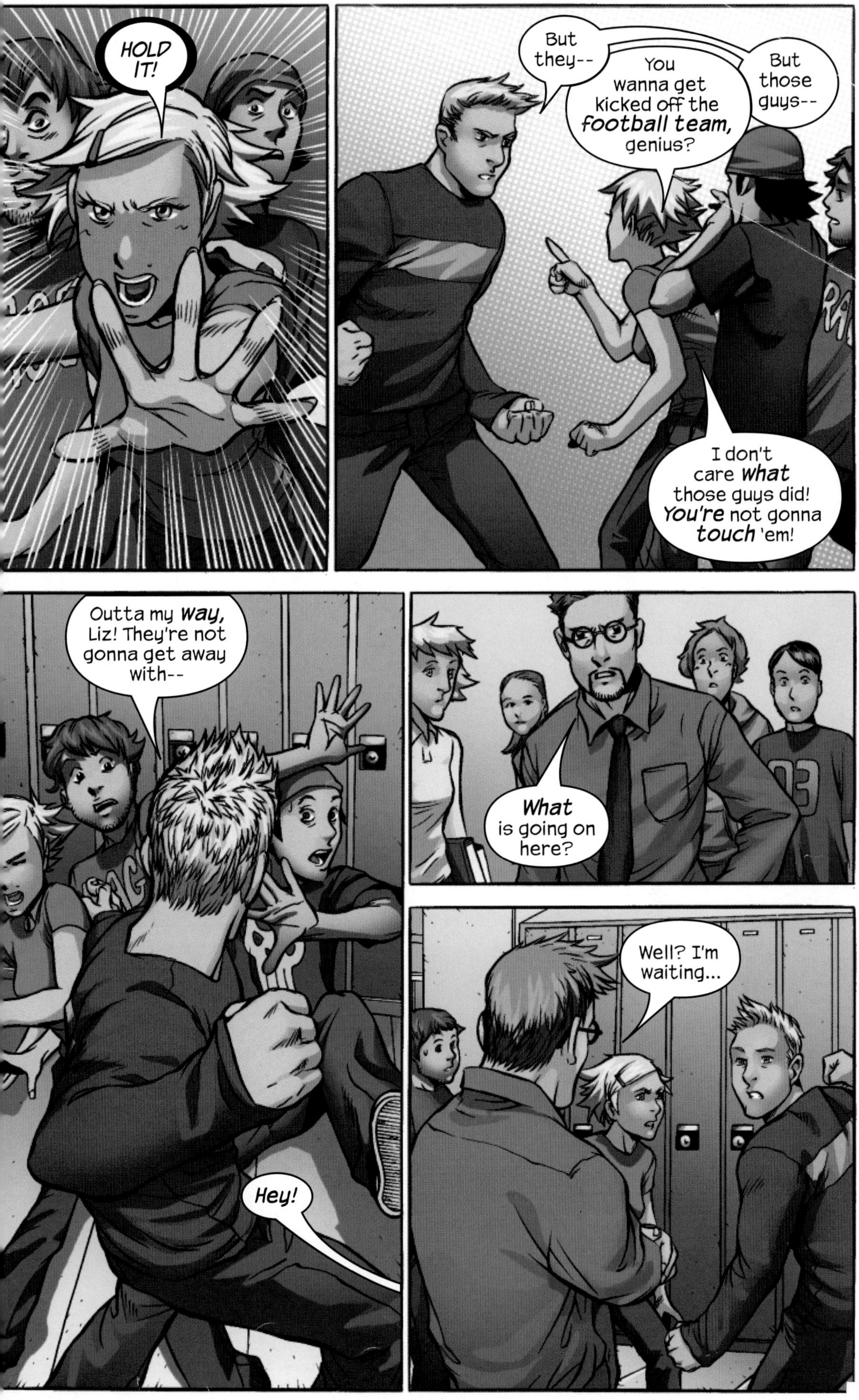
HOLD IT!
But they--
You wanna get kicked off the football team, genius?
But those guys--
I don't care what those guys did! You're not gonna touch 'em!
Outta my way, Liz! They're not gonna get away with--
Hey!
What is going on here?
Well? I'm waiting...

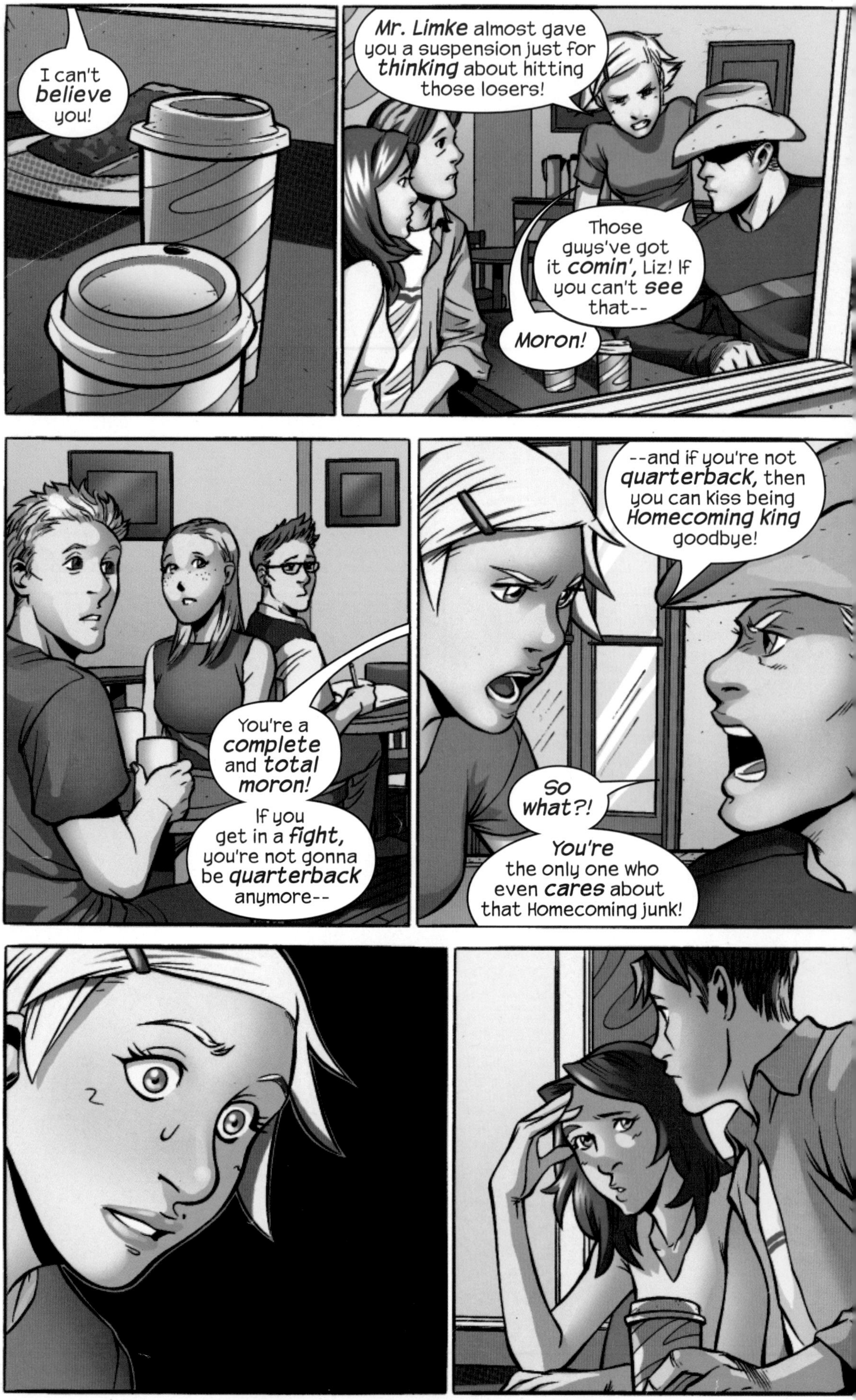
I can't *believe* you!
Mr. Limke almost gave you a suspension just for *thinking* about hitting those losers!
Those guys've got it *comin',* Liz! If you can't *see* that--
Moron!
You're a *complete* and *total moron!*
If you get in a *fight,* you're not gonna be *quarterback* anymore--
--and if you're not *quarterback,* then you can kiss being *Homecoming king* goodbye!
So what?!
You're the only one who even *cares* about that Homecoming junk!

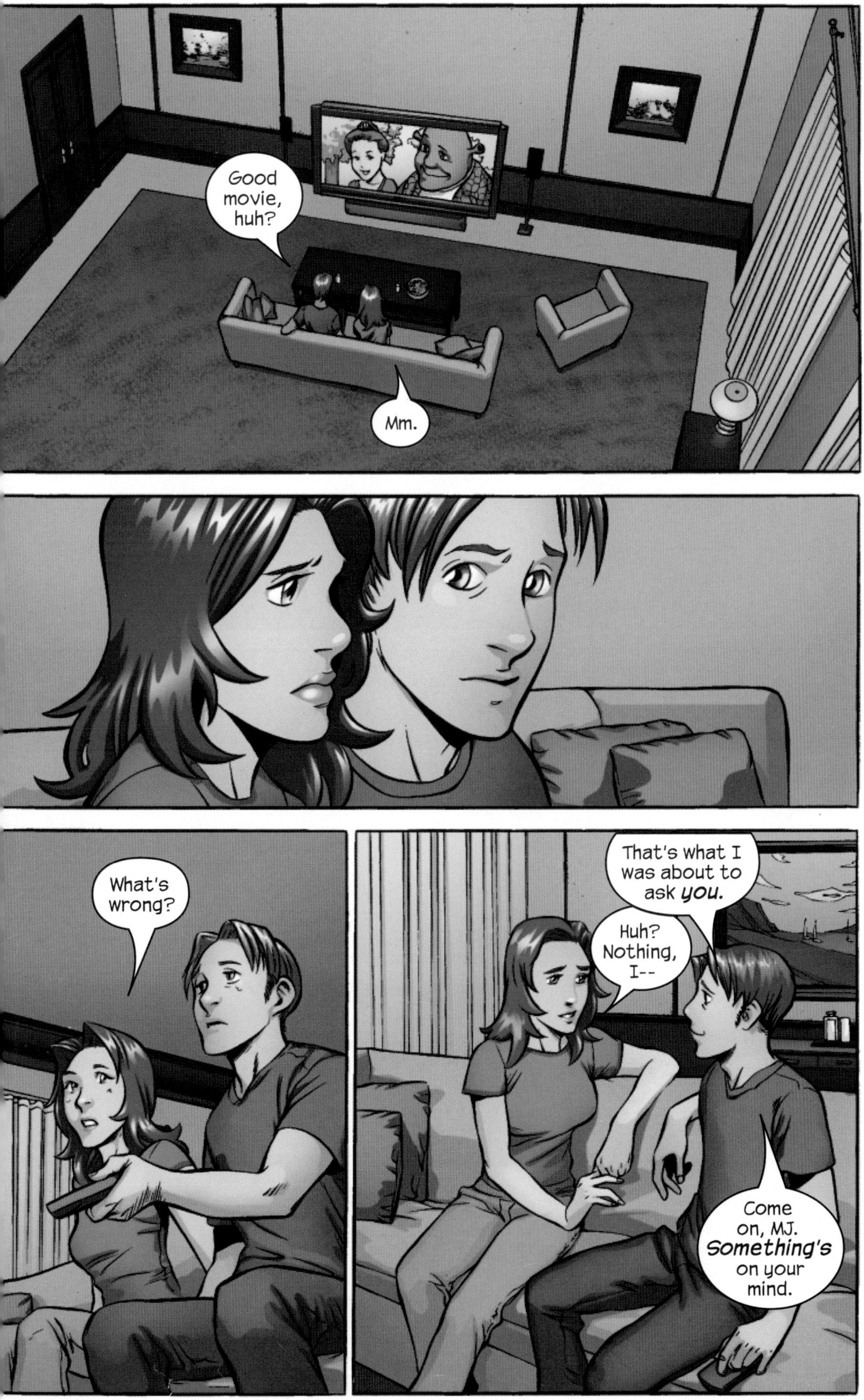
Good movie, huh?
Mm.
What's wrong?
That's what I was about to ask *you.*
Huh? Nothing, I--
Come on, MJ. *Something's* on your mind.

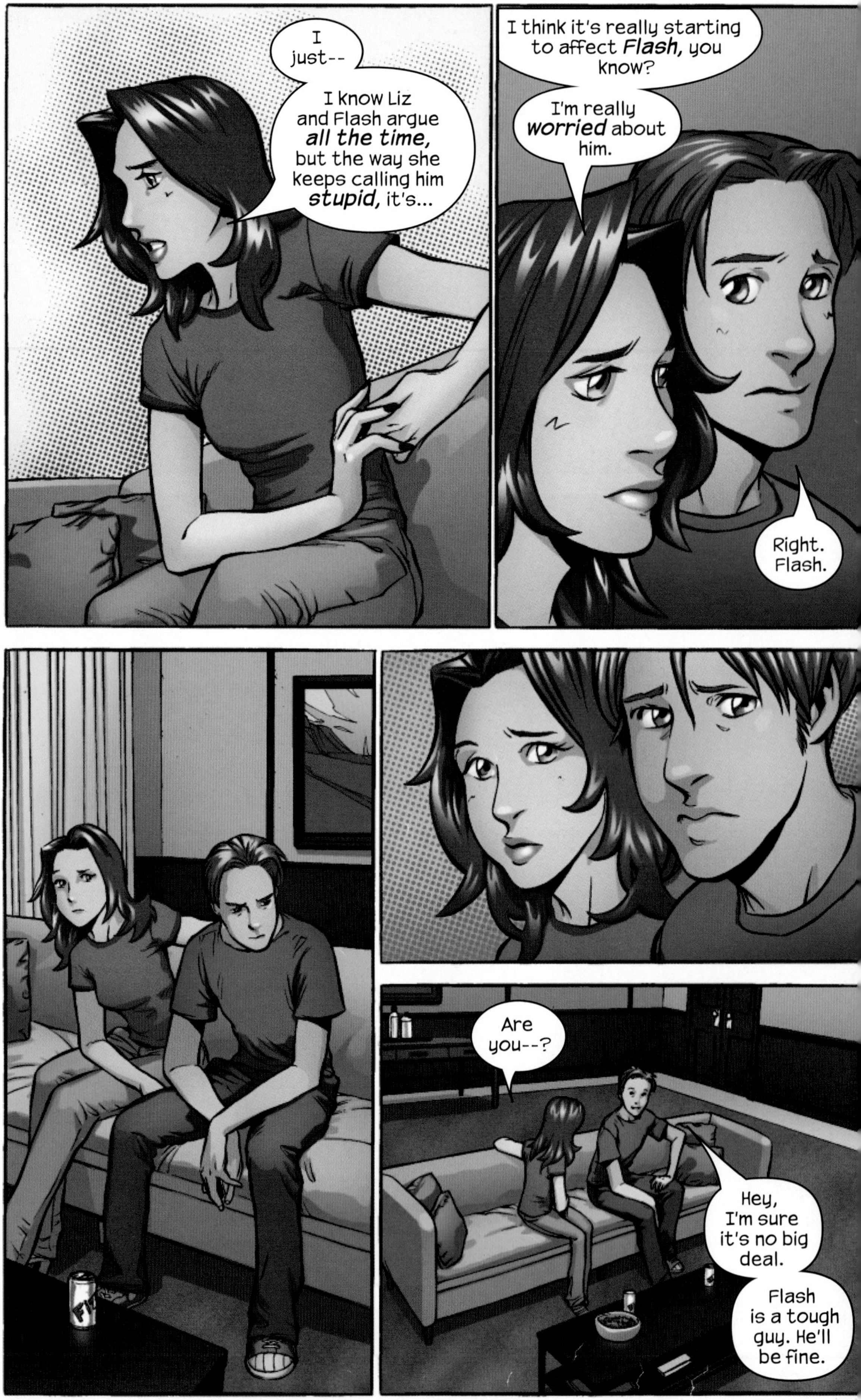
I just--
I know Liz and Flash argue *all the time,* but the way she keeps calling him *stupid,* it's...
I think it's really starting to affect *Flash,* you know?
I'm really *worried* about him.
Right. Flash.
Are you--?
Hey, I'm sure it's no big deal.
Flash is a tough guy. He'll be fine.

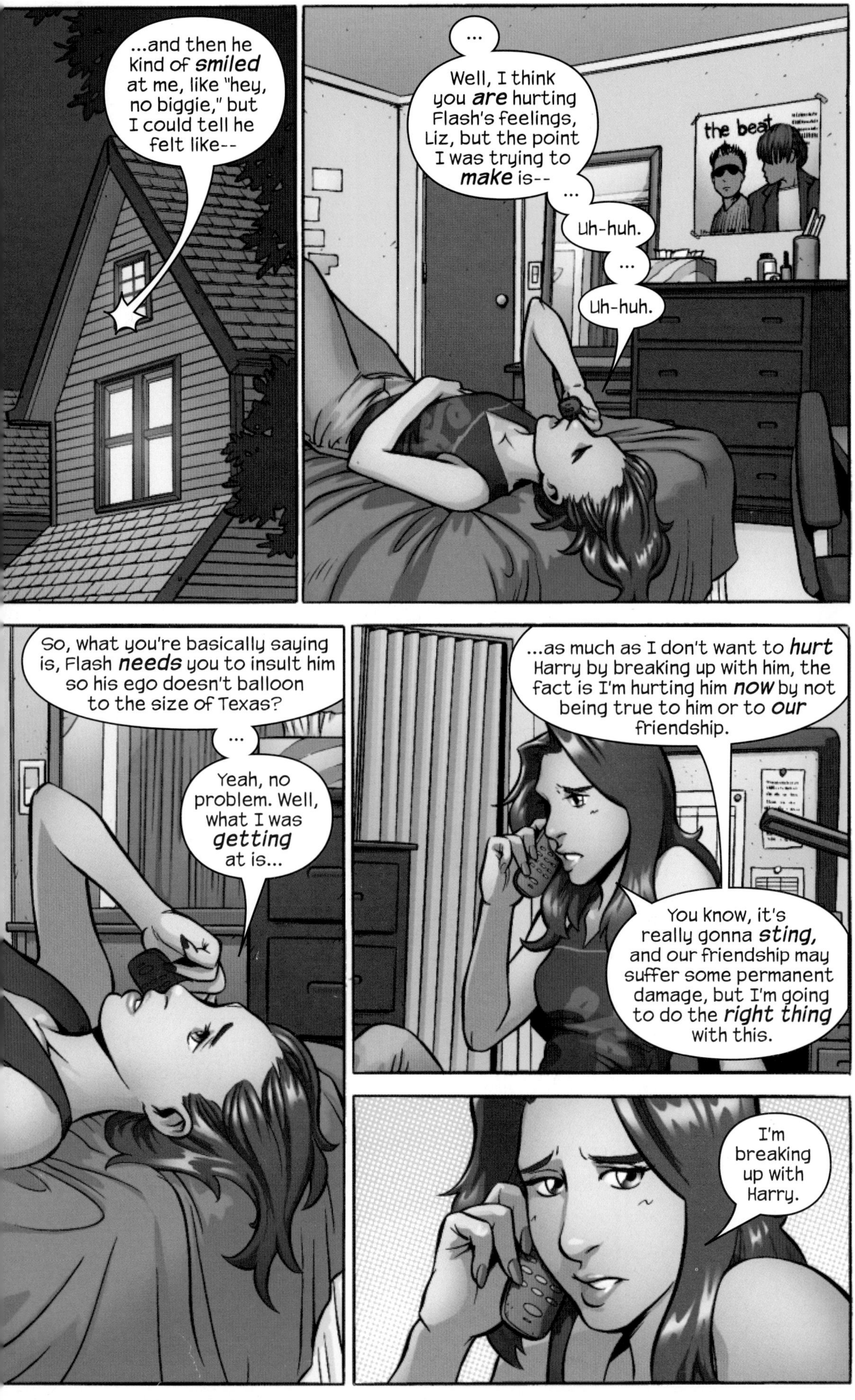
...and then he kind of *smiled* at me, like "hey, no biggie," but I could tell he felt like--
...
Well, I think you *are* hurting Flash's feelings, Liz, but the point I was trying to *make* is--
...
Uh-huh.
...
Uh-huh.
the beat
So, what you're basically saying is, Flash *needs* you to insult him so his ego doesn't balloon to the size of Texas?
...
Yeah, no problem. Well, what I was *getting* at is...
...as much as I don't want to *hurt* Harry by breaking up with him, the fact is I'm hurting him *now* by not being true to him or to *our* friendship.
You know, it's really gonna *sting*, and our friendship may suffer some permanent damage, but I'm going to do the *right thing* with this.
I'm breaking up with Harry.

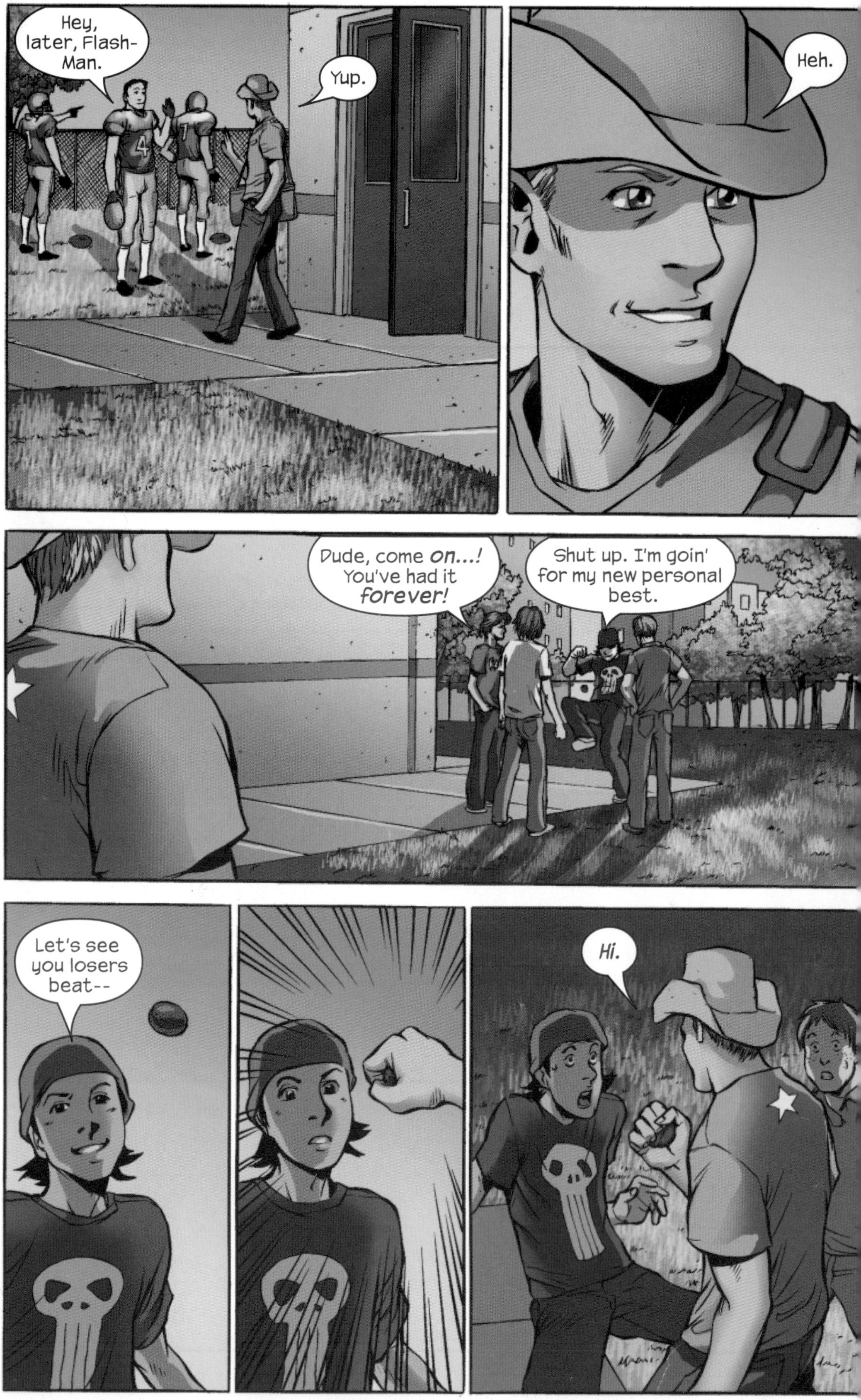
Hey, later, Flash-Man.
Yup.
Heh.
Dude, come *on*...! You've had it *forever!*
Shut up. I'm goin' for my new personal best.
Let's see you losers beat--
Hi.

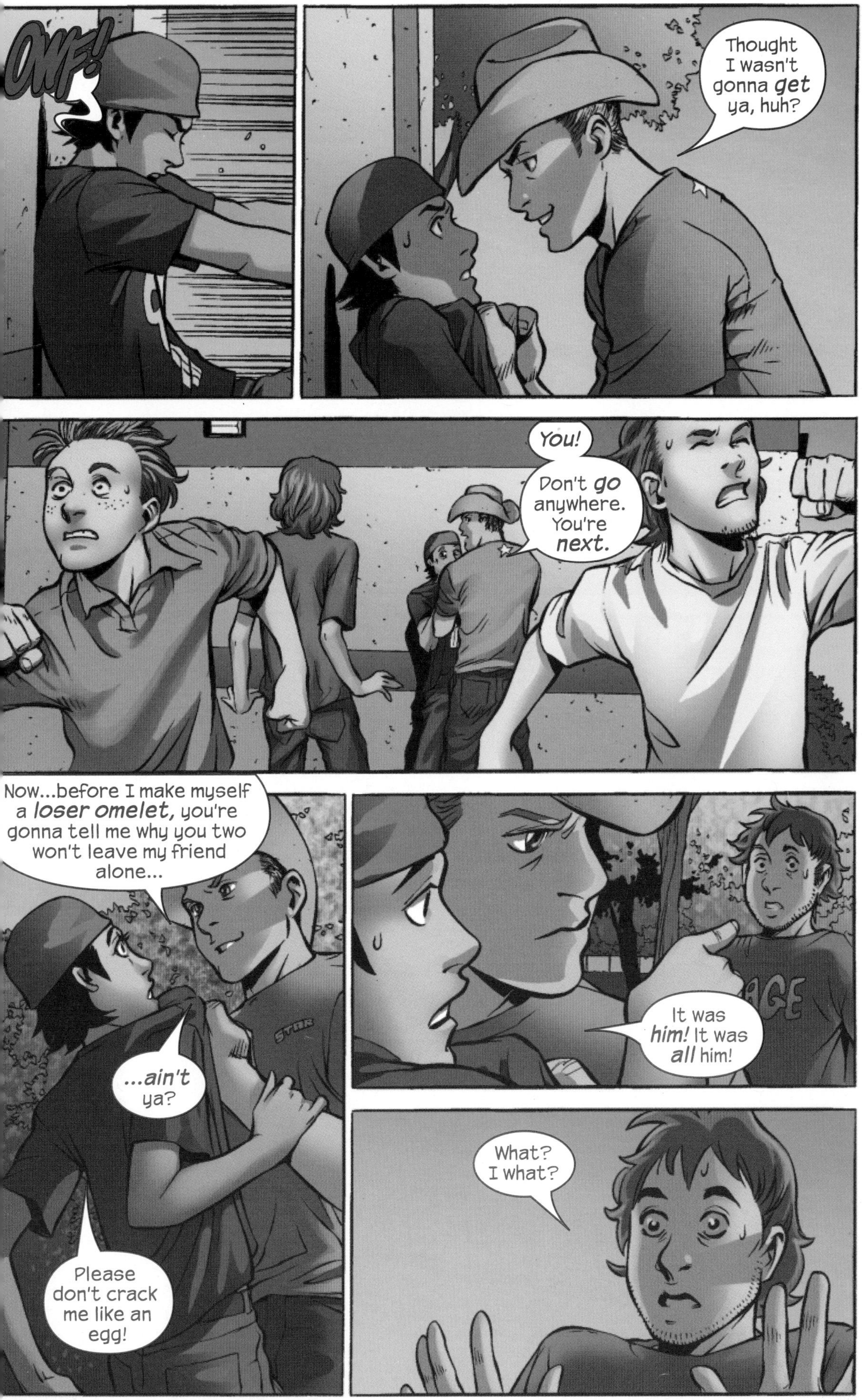
OWF!
Thought I wasn't gonna get ya, huh?
You!
Don't go anywhere. You're next.
Now...before I make myself a loser omelet, you're gonna tell me why you two won't leave my friend alone...
...ain't ya?
Please don't crack me like an egg!
It was him! It was all him!
What? I what?

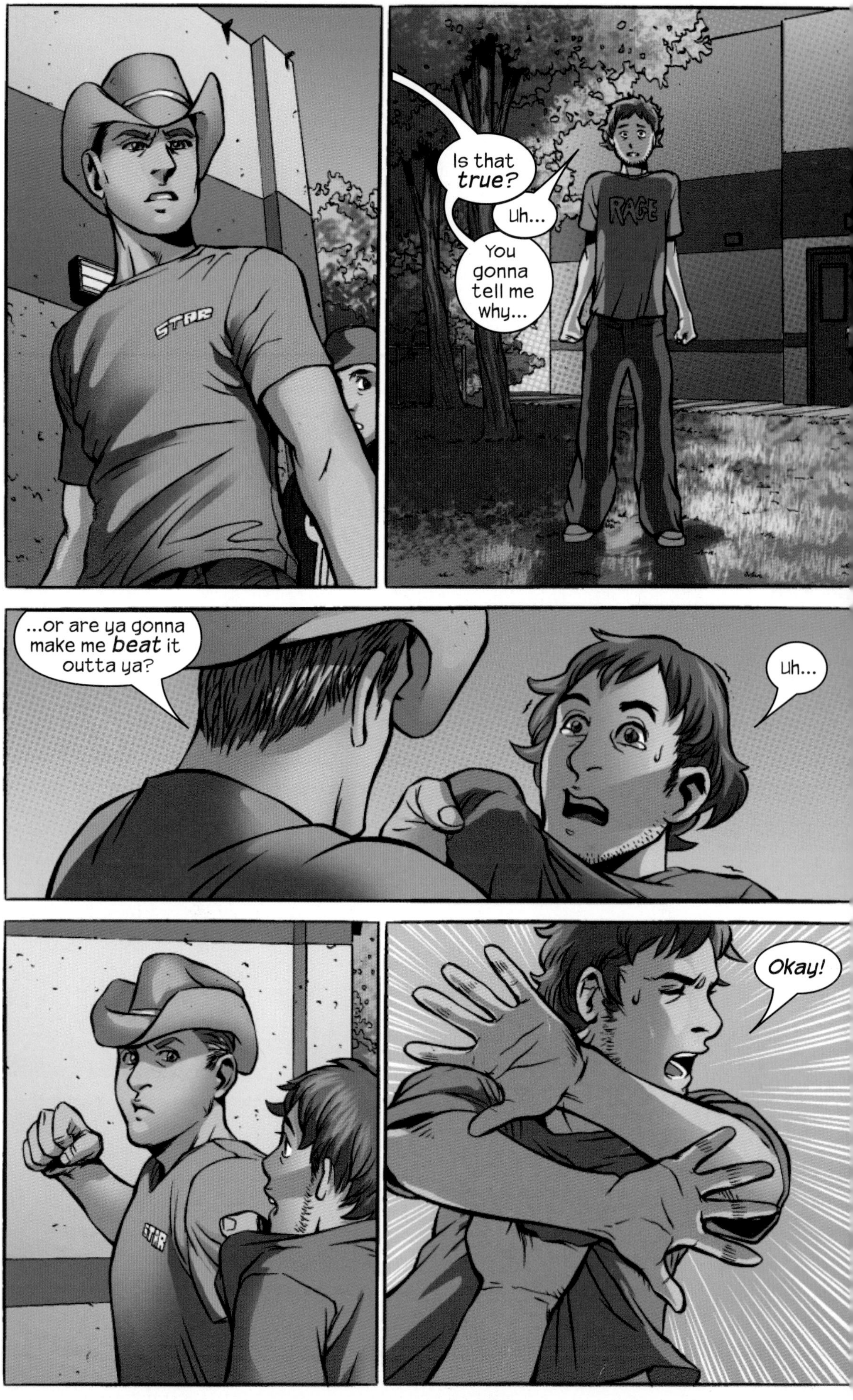
Is that true?
Uh...
You gonna tell me why...
...or are ya gonna make me beat it outta ya?
Uh...
Okay!

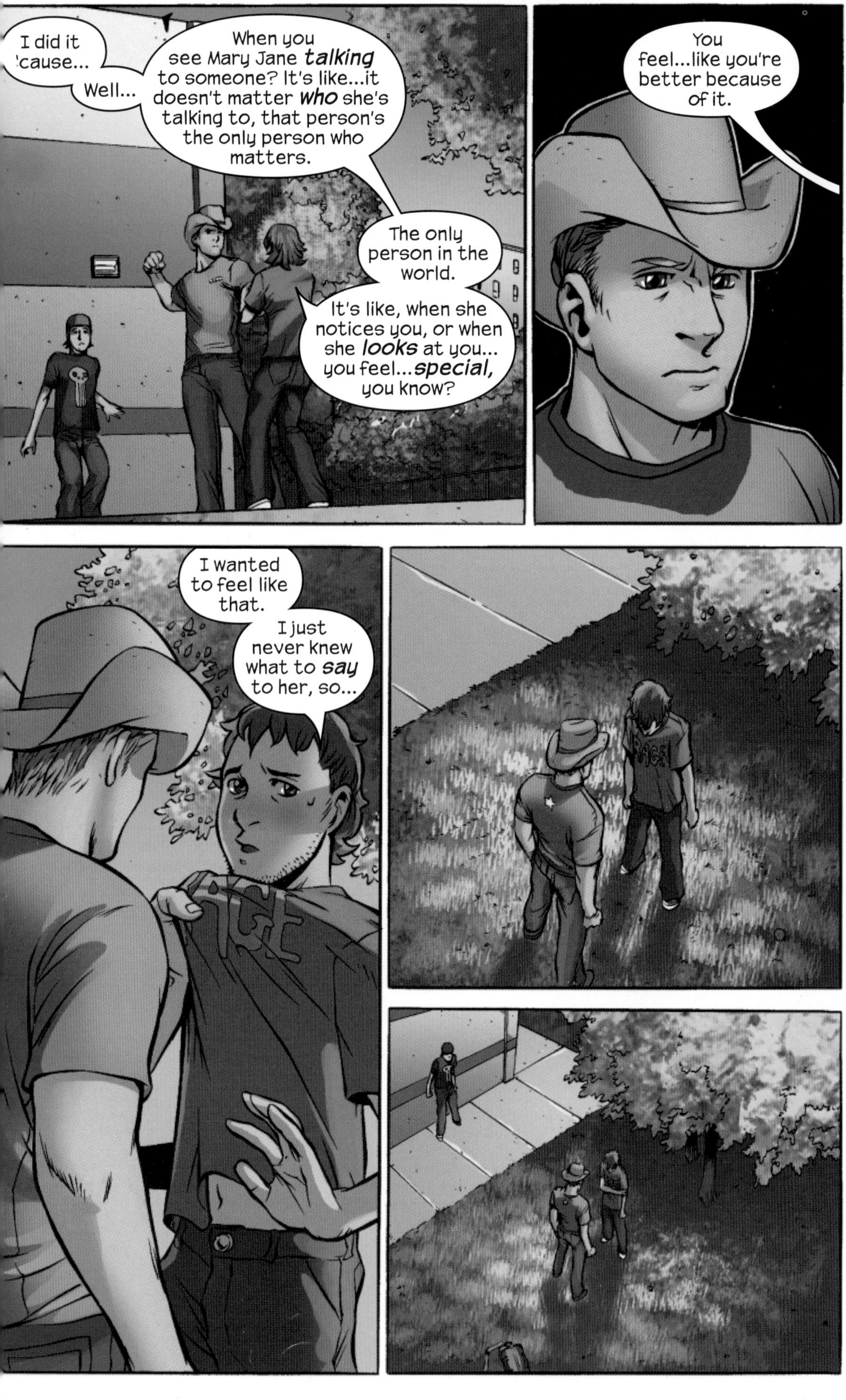

I did it 'cause...
Well...
When you see Mary Jane talking to someone? It's like...it doesn't matter who she's talking to, that person's the only person who matters.
The only person in the world.
It's like, when she notices you, or when she looks at you... you feel...special, you know?
You feel...like you're better because of it.
I wanted to feel like that.
I just never knew what to say to her, so...

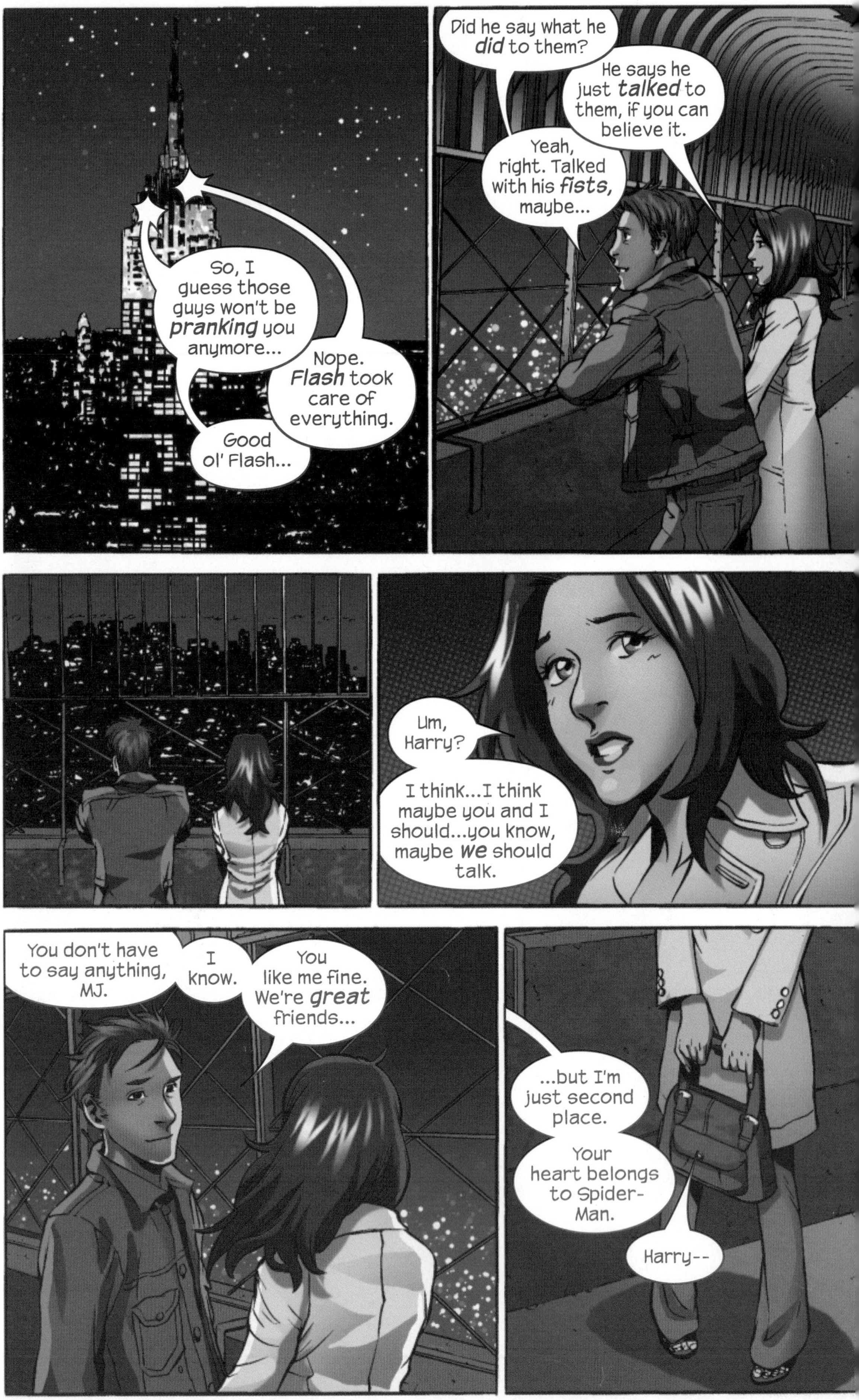

So, I guess those guys won't be *pranking* you anymore...
Nope. *Flash* took care of everything.
Good ol' Flash...
Did he say what he *did* to them?
He says he just *talked* to them, if you can believe it.
Yeah, right. Talked with his *fists,* maybe...
Um, Harry?
I think...I think maybe you and I should...you know, maybe *we* should talk.
You don't have to say anything, MJ.
I know.
You like me fine. We're *great* friends...
...but I'm just second place.
Your heart belongs to Spider-Man.
Harry--

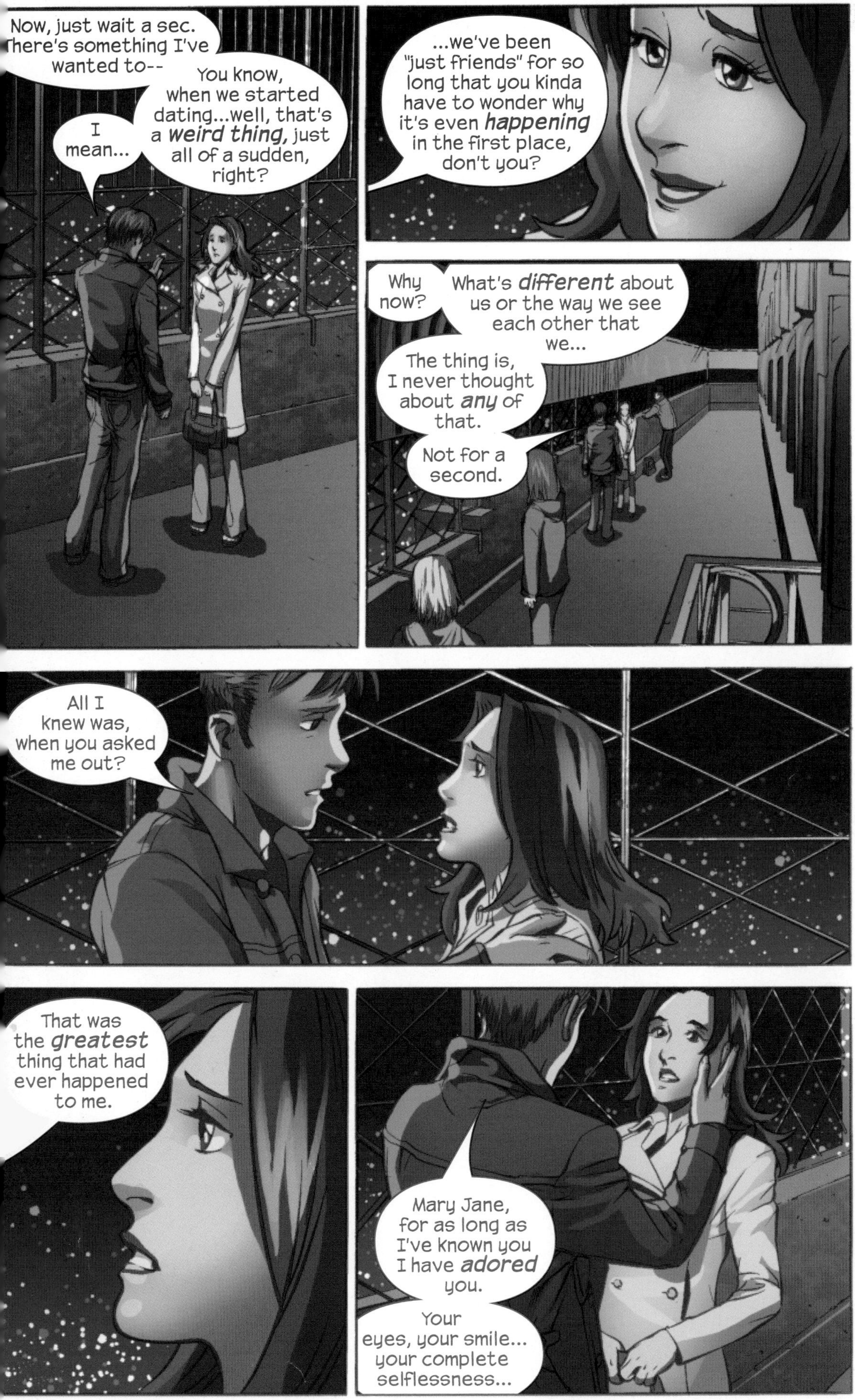
Now, just wait a sec. There's something I've wanted to--
I mean...
You know, when we started dating...well, that's a weird thing, just all of a sudden, right?
...we've been "just friends" for so long that you kinda have to wonder why it's even happening in the first place, don't you?
Why now?
What's different about us or the way we see each other that we...
The thing is, I never thought about any of that.
Not for a second.
All I knew was, when you asked me out?
That was the greatest thing that had ever happened to me.
Mary Jane, for as long as I've known you I have adored you.
Your eyes, your smile... your complete selflessness...

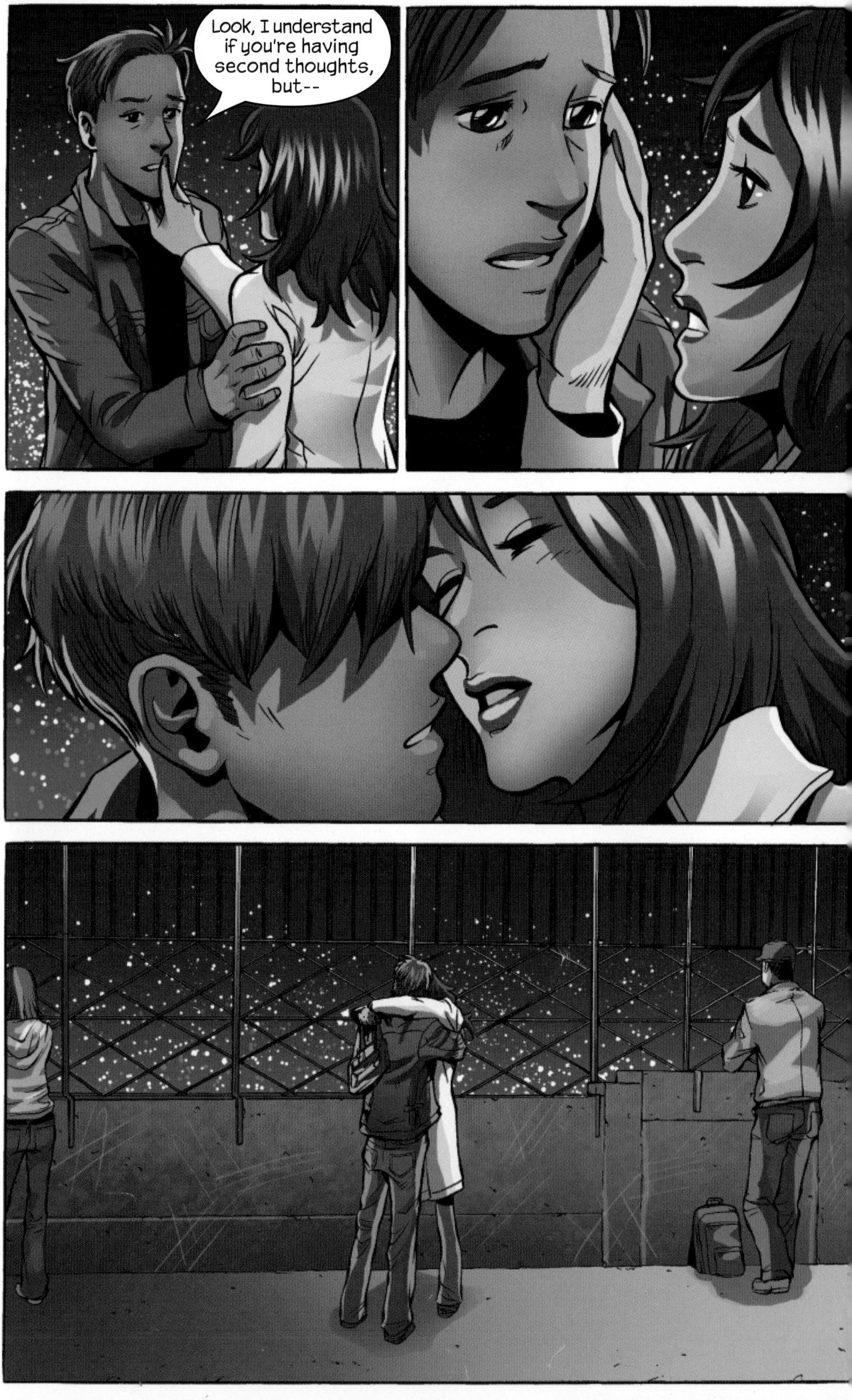
Look, I understand if you're having second thoughts, but--

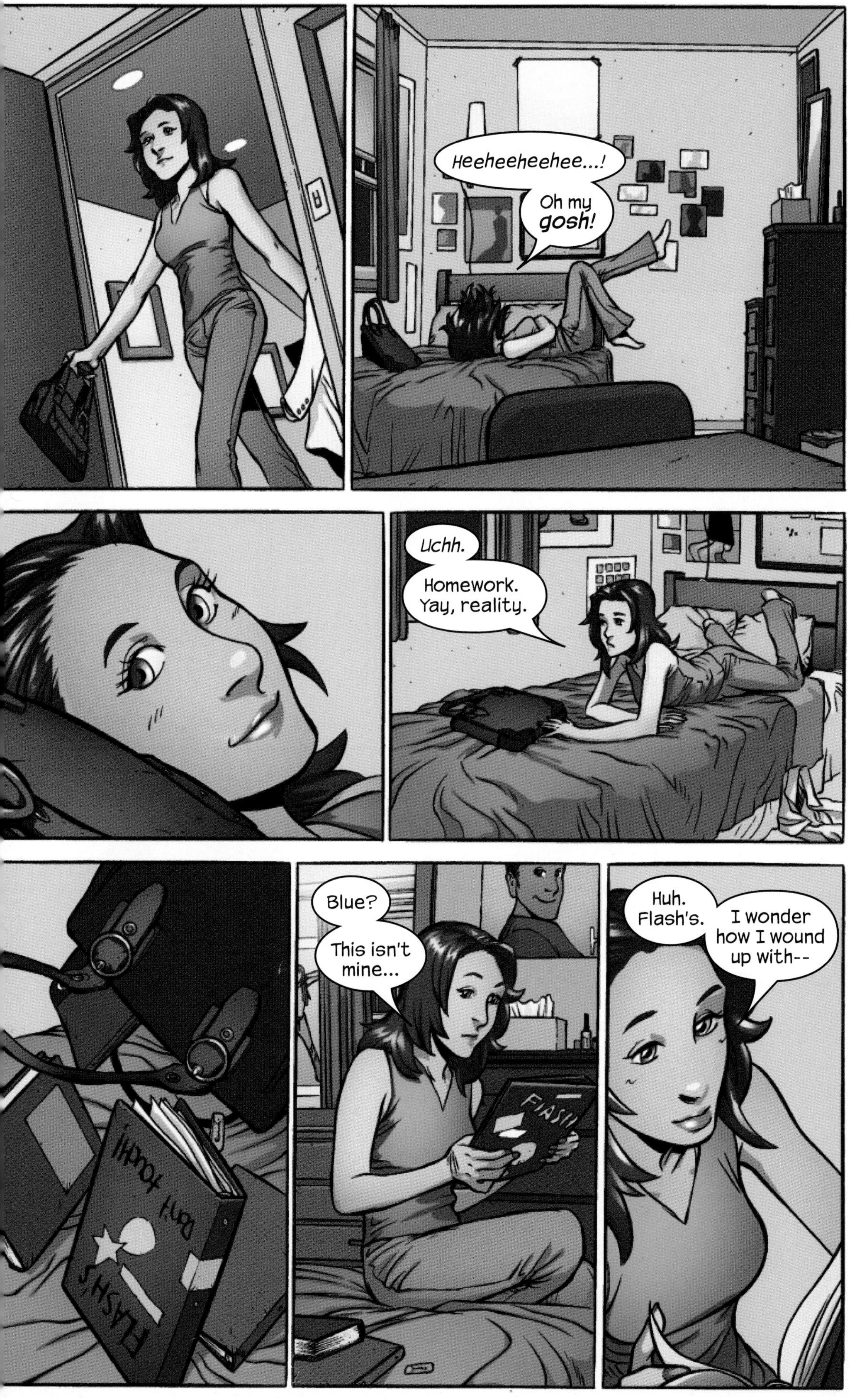
Heeheeheehee...!
Oh my gosh!
Uchh.
Homework. Yay, reality.
FLASH'S Don't touch!!
Blue?
This isn't mine...
FLASH
Huh. Flash's.
I wonder how I wound up with--

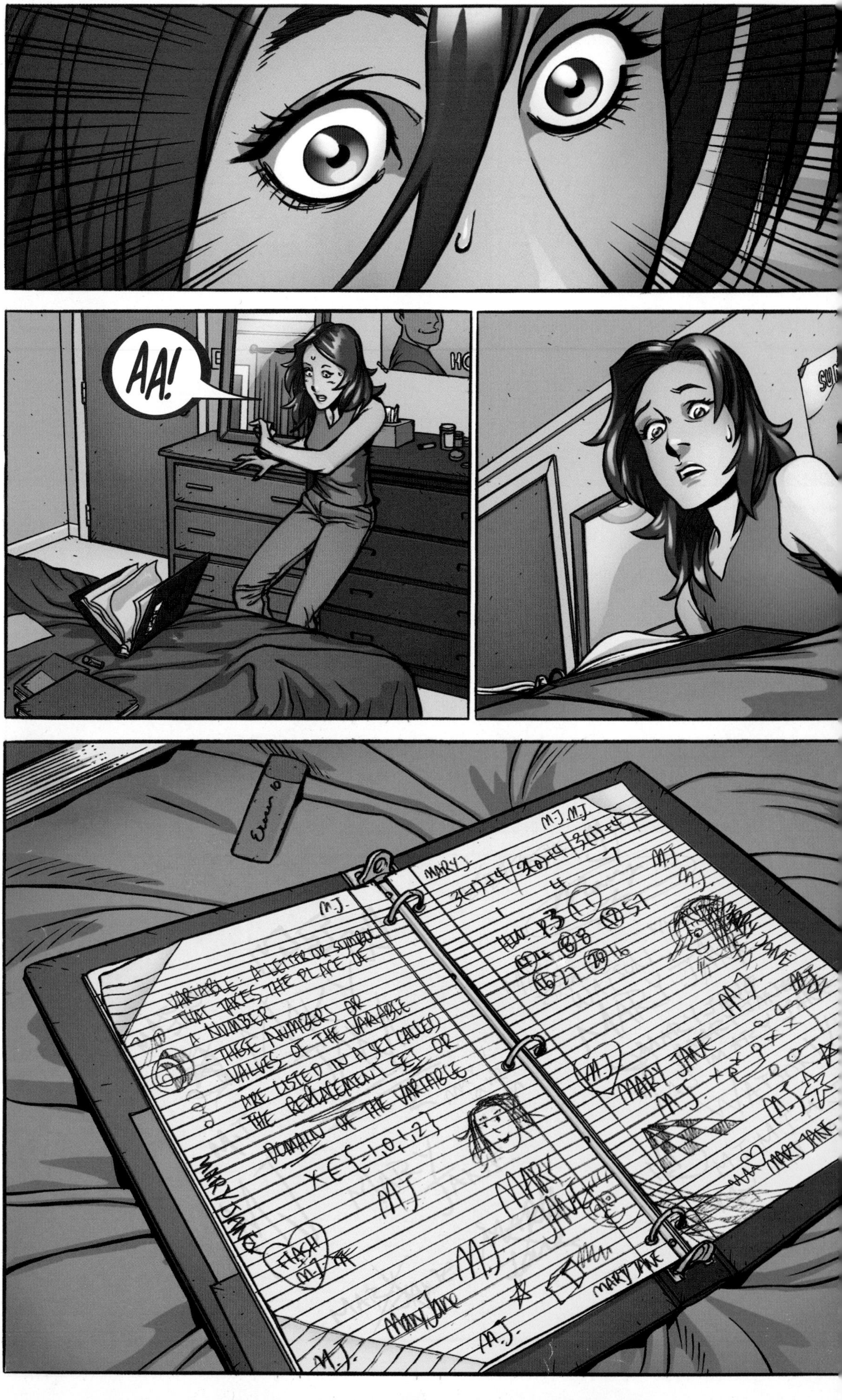
AA!
VARIABLE: A LETTER OR SYMBOL THAT TAKES THE PLACE OF A NUMBER
THESE NUMBERS OR VALUES OF THE VARIABLE ARE LISTED IN A SET CALLED THE REPLACEMENT SET OR DOMAIN OF THE VARIABLE
MARY J.
MARY JANE
M.J.